The Little Green Drum

LIBRARIES NI
WITHDRAWN FROM STOCK

D0812861

There are lots of Early Reader stories you might enjoy.

Look at the back of the book or, for a complete list, visit www.orionbooks.co.uk

The Little Green Drum

Taghreed Najjar

Retold by Lucy Coats

Illustrated by Hassan Manasrah

Orion
Children's Books

Originally published in the Arabic language
in Jordan in 2013
by Al Salwa Publishers
This translated edition first published in Great Britain in 2015
by Orion Children's Books
an imprint of the Hachette Children's Group

Orion House
5 Upper Saint Martin's Lane
London WC2H 9EA
An Hachette UK Company

1 3 5 7 9 10 8 6 4 2

Text © Taghreed Najjar 2013
Illustrations © Hassan Manasrah 2013
Translation © Taghreed Najjar 2013
Retelling © Lucy Coats 2015

The right of Taghreed Najjar and Hassan Manasrah to be identified
as the author and illustrator of this work has been asserted.

All rights reserved. No part of this publication may be reproduced,
stored in a retrieval system, or transmitted, in any form or by any means,
electronic, mechanical, photocopying, recording or otherwise,
without the prior permission of Orion Children's Books.

The Orion Publishing Group's policy is to use papers that are natural,
renewable and recyclable products and made from wood grown in sustainable
forests. The logging and manufacturing processes are expected to conform to
the environmental regulations of the country of origin.

ISBN 978 1 4440 1435 8

A catalogue record for this book is available from the British Library.

Printed and bound in China

www.orionchildrensbooks.co.uk

For my three daughters, Salwa,
Zaina and Karma. T.N.

For all the children touched by war.
May they find peace. L.C.

Contents

Chapter One	11
Chapter Two	23
Chapter Three	31
Chapter Four	39
Chapter Five	55

Chapter One

This is Samia, and this is her dad, Yaba.

Samia and Yaba live in a village called Lifta. All the houses are on the side of a steep hill. Almost every house has a dome on top.

Samia thinks they look like friendly square giants wearing little round hats.

Samia and Yaba know everyone in their village, and everyone knows them. This is because Yaba has a Very Important Job. He is the Dawn Waker-Upper for the whole village, during the holy month of Ramadan.

During Ramadan, no one can eat in the daytime – from when the sun rises at dawn to when it sinks at dusk. Instead, everyone must have an early breakfast.

So Yaba marches around the village in the dark, banging on his drum and shouting:

"Wake up! Wake up, sleepyheads! It's time to eat!"

Samia is proud of Yaba and his Very Important Job. She secretly wishes she could march around the village banging a drum and shouting, just like him.

But when she asks Yaba about it, he laughs.

"There's never been a Dawn Waker-Upper who is a girl, my flower," he says. "Not that I've heard of, anyway."

Samia doesn't know why not. Girls are good at banging drums and shouting too, aren't they?

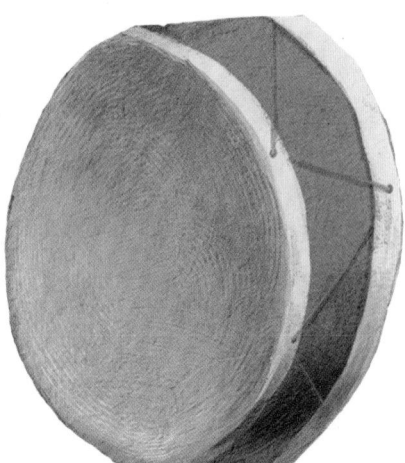

But one year, just before Ramadan, Yaba is not very well.

"Ooh! Ow! Ouch! My poor stomach!" he says. "I think I need to lie down."

Samia brings him a cup of special tummy-ache tea.

"Drink up, Yaba," she says. "You have to be well for tomorrow! It's the first day of Ramadan."

But Yaba doesn't feel better. He doesn't feel better at all. When he tries to get up, he falls back into bed, holding his tummy. It hurts more than ever.

"Oh no!" he moans. "Ramadan will be ruined if I don't wake everyone up!"

Chapter Two

"I can do it, Yaba," says Samia. "I'm strong and brave, and my little green drum is very loud."

"But won't you get lost in the dark?" Yaba asks.

"This lamp is as bright as the stars," says Samia. "It will show me the way."

"But what about the wild wolves?" asks Yaba. "They might eat you."

"Don't worry," says Samia.

"Our dog Barkie is as fierce as a wolf! He'll look after me.

So Yaba stays warm in his bed, and Samia sets off down the rocky road to the village with her little green drum, her bright lamp, and her fierce dog, Barkie.

It is very dark. Samia hums a tune to help her feel brave, and holds her lamp high. But then . . .

Oh no!

She sees two scary, orange eyes shining behind a tree.

What could they be?

Chapter Three

ARROOOOOH!
ARROOOOOOOH!
howls a big, black wolf.

WOOF! WOOF! WOOF! barks Barkie. STAY AWAY FROM SAMIA OR I'LL BITE YOU!

Barkie's growls are so fierce that the big, black wolf runs away.

"Good dog, Barkie!" says Samia, stroking his soft, brown ears. "I knew you'd save me."

She holds up her lamp, and off they go again.

Soon Samia reaches her friend Ahmad's house. She bangs on her little green drum, just like Yaba. Will it work? It **must**!

BOOM -A- BOOM

"Wake up, wake up, sleepyheads! It's time to eat!" she shouts in a loud voice.

Ahmad's dad looks out of the bedroom window.

"Well, I never!" he says. "It's Samia! Where is your Yaba?"

"Yaba is ill and can't get out of bed" says Samia. "So I am taking his place as Dawn Waker-Upper."

"Ooh!" says Ahmad, popping up next to his dad. "I've got a drum.

Can I come too?"

"And me!"

"And me!" say Ahmad's sisters, Ada and Arya.

So Ahmad, Ada and Arya join Samia and Barkie.

BOOM-A-BOOM
BOOM-A-BOOM

"Wake up, wake up sleepyheads! It's time to eat!" they shout.

Chapter Four

Their friend Omar wants to come too.

"I don't have a drum. Can I bring my tambourine?" he asks.

"Why not?" everyone yells.
"Five are louder than four!"

So Omar joins Samia, Barkie, Ahmad, Ada and Arya.

"Wake up, wake up sleepyheads! It's time to eat!" they shout.

BOOM-A-BOOM
BOOM-A-BOOM
JINGLE JANGLE

The next house is Fatima's.

"I don't have a drum or a tambourine. Can I bring my flute?" she asks.

"Why not?" everyone yells.
"Six are louder than five!"

So Fatima joins Samia, Barkie, Ahmad, Ada, Arya and Omar.

BOOM-A-BOOM
BOOM-A-BOOM
JINGLE JANGLE
TOOTLE TOOT

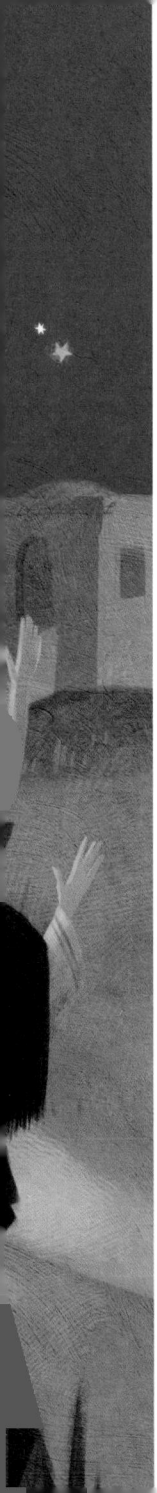

"Wake up, wake up sleepyheads! It's time to eat!" they shout.

"Ooh!" says Adnan when they get to his house.

"I don't have a drum or a tambourine or a flute. Can I bring my lute?"

"Why not?" everyone yells. "Seven are louder than six!"

So Adnan joins Samia, Barkie, Ahmad, Ada, Arya, Omar and Fatima.

BOOM-A-BOOM
BOOM-A-BOOM
JINGLE JANGLE
TOOTLE TOOT
PLINKETY
PLINK

"Wake up, wake up sleepyheads!
It's time to eat!" they shout.

Bahira and Samira are not sure what to bring.
"How about saucepans and spoons?" they ask.

"Why not?" everyone yells. "Nine are loudest of all!"

So Bahira and Samira join Samia, Barkie, Ahmad, Ada, Arya, Omar, Fatima and Adnan.

BOOM-A-BOOM
BOOM-A-BOOM
JINGLE JANGLE
TOOTLE TOOT

PLINKETY
PLINK
BASHETTY
BISH

"Wake up, wake up sleepyheads!
It's time to eat!" they shout.

Chapter Five

Soon Samia has a whole band.

Up and down the village they march, banging and beating, plucking and playing, tooting and hooting.

Then they start to sing.

Bang the drum
along the way
Here we come
Before the day!

Let's give food to everyone,
Eat your meal
Before the sun.
Ramadan is here, hooray!
We **must** eat before the day!

"Surely nobody can still be asleep **now**!" says Samia, giving her little green drum one last **boom-a-boom** to make sure.

Her friends look around. There is a light on in every house.

Everyone in the village is awake.

"Happy Ramadan!" Samia shouts.

"Yes! Happy Ramadan to all the Dawn Waker-Uppers!" say the mums and dads, grannies and granddads, aunties, uncles and cousins.

Samia, Ahmad, Ada, Arya, Omar,
Fatima, Adnan, Bahira and
Samira are given lots of treats.

Samia looks at the sky. The stars are fading. It is nearly dawn.
"I must go home to Yaba," she says. "I hope his tummy-ache has gone."

She waves goodbye to everyone, and she, her little green drum, her bright lamp and her fierce dog, Barkie, walk back up the rocky road.

The big, black wolf is hiding behind a tree. He doesn't dare to come out. Barkie wags his tail happily. He is the Dog King of the village now.

Samia runs into the house.

Yaba is sitting up in bed. He looks much better.

"Welcome home, flower," he says, hugging her. "Is everyone awake?"

"Oh yes, Yaba!" Samia says. "And guess what happened?"

"You'll have to tell me," Yaba says.

So Samia does.

"Happy Ramadan to the best Dawn Waker-Upper in the village," says Yaba, as he and Samia sit down to eat.

"Happy Ramadan to the best Yaba in the whole WORLD," says Samia.

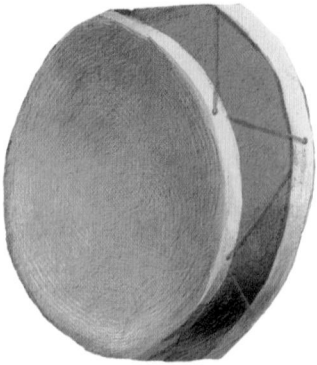

Samia's story happened a long time ago in 1930s Palestine in a village called Lifta. In 1948, there was a war and the villagers of Lifta had to flee to a safer place. When the war ended the villagers were not allowed to return to their homes and today the village still stands empty and unlived in. Taghreed Najjar's family came from Lifta, and she wrote this story in memory of peaceful and happier times there.

In those days, nobody had an alarm clock, so when the holy month of Ramadan came around, every village relied on their Mosaher, or Dawn Waker-Upper to get them up for the early morning meal, which is called Suhoor.

During Ramadan, which falls in the ninth month of the Islamic year, nobody eats between the time the sun rises and sets, so getting a big breakfast in is very important. Muslims also have a Ramadan meal after dark, which is called Iftar.

The end of Ramadan is marked by a big celebration called Eid-ul-Fitr, when Muslims thank Allah for the help and strength that he gives them throughout the month of fasting.

What are you going to read next?

Have more adventures with

Horrid Henry,

or save the day with Anthony Ant!

Become a
superhero with Monstar,

float off to
sea with
Algy,

or have your very own *Pirates' Picnic.*

Grow carrots with

Lottie and Dottie,

make magic with *The Witch Dog,*

and cast a spell with *The Three Little Magicians.*

Enjoy all the Early Readers.

the orion star

CALLING ALL GROWN-UPS!

Sign up for the orion star newsletter to hear about your favourite authors and exclusive competitions, plus details of how children can join our 'Story Stars' review panel.

Sign up at:

www.orionbooks.co.uk/orionstar

Follow us @the_orionstar

Find us facebook.com/TheOrionStar